Summary: Lessons in Chemistry

A Novel

Inspirational Creator

rendering of legal, financial, medical or professional advice. The content within this book has been derived from various sources. Please consult a licensed professional before attempting any techniques outlined in this book.

By reading this document, the reader agrees that under no circumstances is the author responsible for any losses, direct or indirect, that are incurred as a result of the use of the information contained within this document, including, but not limited to, errors, omissions, or inaccuracies.

ISBN 978-1-922940-98-8 (E-book)

ISBN 978-1-922940-99-5 (Paperback)

ISBN 978-1-922940-97-1 (Hardcover)

Cover Design by Byteripper

Published by Inspirational Creator

Edited by Liam Daniels

Written by Alice Moore

First Edition (2023)

Table of Contents

Disclaimer: The following summary is by no means meant to be a replacement for the original text. Any readers are sincerely urged to support the creator, Bonnie Garmus, by reading the original book for the full experience.

YOUR FREE GIFT

As a **thank you** for your purchase, we're offering the book *'The Habits of Highly Joyful People'* completely free.

To get your copy visit inspirationalcreator.com. Alternatively, scan the QR code below.

Get ready to discover:

- the most important source of happiness
- some common myths and misconceptions about happiness
- how to cultivate supportive, loving relationships with one question
- and so much more!

If you want to dig deeper into the science of happiness, make sure to grab the free book.

In addition to the GIFT, you'll also have access to exclusive giveaways, discounts, and other valuable information.

Introduction

This is a comprehensive summary of the No. 1 Global Bestseller to aid readers in their understanding and experience, with insightful additions and page references to the original.

In the narrow-minded 1960s, Elizabeth Zott is a sharp-witted and deeply undervalued chemist among her male colleagues. After being unfairly fired, she hesitantly becomes the host of a cooking show targeted at the average housewife, *Supper at Six*. Only she doesn't set out to pleasantly smile and make cocktails, but rather to introduce her female audience to the world of science and chemistry.

Her journey starts when she meets her chemical and romantic match, Calvin Evans. Together they navigate the rocky terrain of scientific research, relationships, cumbersome coworkers, and rowing until their love story is prematurely cut short, and Elizabeth and their intelligent dog, Six-thirty, are left to pick up the pieces.

However, there are things that even the brilliant Elizabeth doesn't know about her significant other, as secrets and mysteries start to unravel from his haunted past. Unbeknownst to her, another surprise that he had left for her is just on the way.

Suddenly, she's fired from the only field of work she'd ever prided herself in and left at an impasse. Until she meets Walter, an anxious producer with an impending deadline to find a TV star, which he does—in Elizabeth. Her show, *Supper at Six*, captivates America with science-based nutritional meals and strict chemistry lessons but also infuriates the close-minded populace and the show's executive producer.

Having dealt with being spoken over and unrecognized her entire life, especially in her groundbreaking chemical research, she has always prevailed in the face of adversity. But this time, it'll take more than sheer will and self-determination to overcome her severe depression.

With the help of her unlikely found family consisting of Walter, her neighbor, a coxswain, her literate dog, and a minister, she must find the strength to start each day anew and prove, with scientific precision, that all who've doubted her are wrong.

Chapter 1: November 1961

Elizabeth Zott, the no-nonsense, thirty-year-old mother of five-year-old Madeline Zott, was making her daughter's school lunch. The two lived in Commons, which was described to be as drab as its name, a Southern Californian town in the 1960s.

Elizabeth, despite being severely depressed, ensured to write instructions in her daughter's lunch every day, telling her how to fit in—but not too much. She wrote on the note to not let the boys win too easily in sports and that almost everyone is awful.

Madeline could read these notes with ease as she was incredibly intelligent, with a reading ability far ahead of her peers, but she kept this to herself at school to not draw attention. She knew her talent would only irritate people because her classmates would eventually catch up to her reading level anyway.

As Elizabeth drives off to her job as the host of the cooking show *Supper at Six*, it's clear something happened to her in her past and that she's deeply unhappy because of it.

The two-page chapter is unusually short for an introduction but provides just enough information to leave readers with one burning question: What happened to the mysterious Elizabeth Zott?

Chapter 2: Pine

New characters

- Calvin Evans: someone linked to Elizabeth's past

- Walter Pine: Amanda's TV producer father

- Amanda Pine: the girl stealing Madeline's lunch

It's apparent that Madeline felt alienated in school because of her gifts, and so she tried to buy friendship with a girl named Amanda Pine. The price? Madeline's home-cooked lunch that was specially made by her mom to fulfill the nutrients needed for a growing girl. This went on for a time until Elizabeth noticed Madeline's unusual weight loss and went to confront Amanda's father, Walter Pine, at his workplace after her calls had been continuously ignored.

He happened to be a TV show producer and was startled by Elizabeth's bluntness and beauty. She spoke to him like she was the boss, despite him initially assuming she was auditioning for a nurse, and lectured him on the importance of giving his daughter her own food for her development.

Elizabeth was a chemist at the Hastings Research Institute, but after her display in front of Mr. Pine, a new job opportunity arose. She had mentioned the concept of teaching the country how to make food with purpose, and thus, *Supper at Six* was born. Her abysmal pay as a chemist due to her being a woman meant she was quick to drop it for the higher-paying TV show, however, embarrassed it made her feel.

Her straightforward approach to food as a science and making large, wholesome meals made her a fan favorite and earned her the belittling nickname "Luscious Lizzie." This meant her fame wasn't even accredited to her real name. However, all was not well in Elizabeth's life, and readers take note of a new character that was supposedly part of how everything began: Calvin Evans.

Themes of loneliness are revealed in this chapter, with Madeline's genius making it difficult to make friends and Elizabeth's depression linked to Calvin Evans, which will be explored further in the next chapter.

Chapter 3: Hastings Research Institute

New and revised characters

- Calvin Evans: a famous chemist and rower

- Dr. Donatti: Elizabeth and Calvin's boss at Hastings

- Dr. Meyers: Elizabeth's ex-thesis-advisor at the University of California

Ten years earlier, Calvin Evans, an introverted genius, grudge-holder, and rower, chose to work in Commons because it hardly ever rained, and his many other offers were based in wetter climates.

He was a teenage prodigy and now furthered his chemical research at the Hastings Research Institute, where Elizabeth also worked at the time.

He'd been given his own large lab, while everyone, less famous or not a man, worked in cramped spaces and had a shortage of supplies. Because of this, Elizabeth took the initiative and strolled into his lab, past the various no-entry signs, to take some beakers she needed for her research.

Their first meeting was unpleasant, with Calvin assuming she was a secretary, which she responded to by taking the beakers without his permission. Calvin tried to ask her out the next time they met, but with his little dating experience and her disinterest, she declined.

Her colleagues were angry when they learned how she'd treated the famous chemist and said horrible things behind her back. A certain word triggered Elizabeth, who was traumatized as a graduate student at the University of California.

In a flashback to the trauma, she'd found a problem with a test while alone with her thesis advisor, Dr. Meyers, late at night. She asked him about it, but he shrugged off her concerns and called her that same word. He tried to sexually assault her, but she managed to stab him in self-defense with a nearby pencil. The police didn't believe her, and it resulted in her being kicked out with a fabricated story to protect Meyers.

This is why she still wears a pencil in her hair in present-day.

Presently, Elizabeth was assigned to a different research topic than the one she was nearly finalizing. Her boss, Dr. Donatti, who'd called her that triggering word, had made the decision.

Two weeks later, Elizabeth was at the theater, coincidentally at the same time Calvin was on a date. After Elizabeth's disagreement with the play and Calvin's stomach's disagreement with the food he ate, they collided, and Calvin vomited on her. But Elizabeth didn't seem fazed by this and helped him get home safely.

The pair met again, and Elizabeth explained her research topic—Abiogenesis, the theory that life originated from non-living forms, which she was reassigned from. A disagreement arose when Elizabeth mentioned that sexism was likely the cause for reallocation, but Calvin was oblivious to any discrimination or notion that women would even want to work in science.

He offered to involve himself so that Donatti would have to rethink his decision. Elizabeth was initially against this favor, but after Calvin prompted her to make the system work to her advantage instead of falling victim, she agreed. The two swore a strictly work-related partnership, but they both secretly hoped otherwise.

Chapter 4: Introduction to Chemistry

After weeks of working together, Elizabeth and Calvin were fighting in a parking lot over a misunderstanding. Elizabeth had tried to make the romantic feelings she'd developed for him clear with a silkworm metaphor, which Calvin misinterpreted as her saying she wasn't interested in him.

It wasn't long after being separated that Calvin knocked on her car window, and Elizabeth acted on her repressed feelings by kissing him.

They were both interested and irritated by one another, which made it hard to stay apart. They bickered over misaligning views and misunderstandings, but with their love for chemistry and their strong pull to each other after their first meeting, it was clear that they were soulmates.

The two would begin to grow together: Calvin learning from his past ignorance, and Elizabeth slowly overcoming her inability to accept help, both of which will be seen more in coming chapters.

Chapter 5: Family Values

New characters

- Calvin's Father: a mysterious character

- John Zott: Elizabeth's deceased brother

Rumors spread as Elizabeth and Calvin began dating, speculating that they were using each other for her looks or his fame, but this was wrong as they were closer than ever.

One night after sleeping together, Calvin mentioned the topic of family, which they'd never discussed before. Calvin revealed that he had a very hard childhood; orphaned at the age of five after a train accident and put into a Catholic orphanage when his aunt died in a car crash a year later.

This left Elizabeth with many questions about how he could afford to attend Cambridge after growing up in an orphanage or learn to row, but she didn't pry as it was her turn to talk about her past.

Elizabeth's father was a religious con man, and her mother made the props that fooled people into giving him money. He used pistachios to create fire as a "convenient sign from God" (Garmus, 2022, p. 37) to help sell the con, which was how Elizabeth got interested in chemistry.

She wasn't on good terms with her family, and Calvin

couldn't understand why, as he'd always wanted one of his own. Elizabeth explained that her brother, John, had committed suicide at seventeen after her father verbally abused and shunned him because he was gay.

After his death, she'd educated herself at the library because her family moved too often for her to attend school. Both of her parents fled because they'd committed tax evasion, with her father now in prison due to a stunt gone wrong, and her mother remarried in Brazil.

Calvin opened up on what he used to tell himself as a child to give him hope: that "every day was new" (Garmus, 2022, p. 40). This becomes very important in later chapters.

He suddenly remembered something relating to his father, which caused him to stop the conversation. They both lied and said they'll talk about it more the next day.

Their pasts gave more insight into their characters, with Calvin's abandonment issues—which will resurface later—and Elizabeth being forced to grow up too soon, explaining her extreme independence. Both had lost their childhood innocence, and their past was too painful to relive, leading to them suppressing it again.

It's clear that Calvin doesn't tell Elizabeth everything, especially more about his father, the truth of which will be revealed soon.

Chapter 6: The Hastings Cafeteria

New characters

- Miss Frask: a secretary at Hastings

The chapter is told from the perspective of Elizabeth and Calvin's colleagues in the cafeteria: three geologists and a secretary named Miss Frask. The group is jealous of the happy couple, despite Miss Frask and a geologist called Eddie dating and preying on their downfall.

They sneered at Calvin's third Nobel Peace Prize nomination, then at Elizabeth's homemade lunch, and finally at the ring Calvin placed on the table.

The couple was living together, despite it being frowned upon that Elizabeth was unmarried, with the agreement that she would pay her half with a home-cooked dinner because her salary couldn't cover it. Elizabeth mentioned being a stand-in bridesmaid for a friend's wedding, which Calvin took as an opportunity to propose.

However, Elizabeth had made her stance that she'd never marry clear. If they married, she feared that her accomplishments would then be linked to Calvin's surname, losing her individual identity. Furthermore, she vowed off marriage because of her thrice-remarried misogynistic mother's views: that no woman could refuse marriage.

Calvin failed to understand the reasons for her rejection and hypocritically shut down the idea of changing his surname to hers because of his image. He stated that he no longer wanted to marry her but tried bringing up the idea of being a family once more, which Elizabeth misunderstood as meaning having a child. He meant a dog, which Elizabeth happily accepted, leaving the group cheering for their break-up disappointed.

This chapter reaffirmed Elizabeth's views on marriage and having children, which she believed to be synonymous with female oppression and dependence. She wanted to be her own person, given recognition for her hard work and not her partner's name, but Calvin mentioned in Chapter 3 that this was near impossible for a woman to do in their time. He believed she should use his connections to her advantage alongside her research, but she saw this as a form of dependence.

If you are enjoying this book so far, it would mean a lot to me if you could take a minute to review or rate it on the respective platform you acquired it from. Did you know that just 0.5 - 1% of readers do actually end up leaving a review? Thank you :)

Chapter 7: Six-Thirty

New characters

- Six-Thirty: Elizabeth and Calvin's found ex-bomb-sniffer dog

- The coxswain, Dr. Mason: commander of the boat of rowers and an obstetrician, a medical professional focused on pregnancy and childbirth

After a dog followed Elizabeth home at 6:30 p.m., and she mistakenly called out the time when Calvin asked who the dog was, the dog became part of the family. He was very intelligent, picking up commands easily because he was previously a bomb-sniffer dog. Six-thirty, as he was named, couldn't bring himself to find and sacrifice himself on the deadly bombs, unlike the simpler German Shepards. Because of this, he was abandoned and terrified of loud noises.

Six-thirty is portrayed as anthropomorphic, meaning he's given the human characteristic of having his own thoughts, which are revealed only to the reader throughout the book.

Calvin now had the family he'd always wanted and was determined to get Elizabeth into rowing next. Elizabeth was uninterested, but Calvin implied that it was because she thought "women *can't* row" (Garmus, 2022, p. 62).

She had to prove him wrong, so they arrived at a

boathouse where Calvin started practicing on an erg, an indoor rowing machine. The coxswain and a group of eight rowers entered, confronted with Calvin in their way. The coxswain began screaming orders and crude motivation at him, putting him into a hyper-focused trance. Calvin was mentally and physically exhausted afterward but still managed to introduce Elizabeth as his rowing partner.

With the added pressure of being known as Calvin Evans's rowing partner, Elizabeth couldn't back out.

Calvin had helped Elizabeth come out of her comfort zone. Her determination to be viewed as an equal and to perpetuate the idea that women can do anything created a new passion for rowing, which soon became a very important part of her life.

Chapter 8: Overreaching

New characters

- The rich sponsor: mysteriously funds Hastings with the sole interest of abiogenesis

- Dr. Boryweitz: Elizabeth's anxious colleague

Days of training in the two-seater boat, known as a pair, passed with no progress. The eight-seater boat was supposedly easier to row, but Calvin thought she'd never be accepted in the all-male group because she was an amateur and a woman. But after Elizabeth reduced her understanding of rowing to science formulae, she started rapidly improving, despite her not knowing how to swim.

Although, as she progressed in rowing, she regressed in her research, as Donatti said she wasn't smart enough to continue and canceled her project.

The next part of the chapter is portrayed from Donatti's perspective, revealing his hatred and jealousy of Calvin and his misogynistic views. He hatched a plan to take revenge on Calvin by trying to romance Elizabeth and started by insulting her intelligence to lower her self-esteem, which never worked.

After her research was rejected by Donatti again, Elizabeth talked to a fellow frustrated lab worker, Dr. Boryweitz, over their joint feelings of hopelessness.

Her project was still canceled after several weeks, and Calvin couldn't help but involve himself without her knowing. Calvin threatened that he would leave, taking with him his fame and investor funding. Donatti would have been fine with this if it weren't for a mysterious big-league sponsor who'd suddenly appeared, interested only in abiogenesis—Elizabeth's research subject.

Elizabeth was ecstatic that her research was no longer canceled, which she thought was due to her own persistence.

Calvin went on to involve himself again, trying to convince the coxswain to let Elizabeth row in the eight-seater. The coxswain, Dr. Mason, was an obstetrician and knew the resilience of women but was unsure until Calvin used himself as a bargaining chip, saying he would row with them if she could too.

Calvin misled Elizabeth and told her that her sudden acceptance was because they were impressed by her rowing. He knew she couldn't swim even if she'd failed to tell him and knew an eight-seater would be safer for her.

Because everyone he'd ever cared for had died, Calvin was convinced that he was to blame and was a catalyst for bad luck. He was consumed by the thought of Elizabeth dying too, which manifested in him trying to save her from everything, even when he knew she would despise it. This may stem from his abandonment issues, making him obsessive and overprotective so as to not lose another loved one.

On the car ride back home, Elizabeth mentioned the grudge-holding that Calvin was infamous for, which she'd never seen. He said he couldn't think of anyone he held a lifelong grudge against. This statement will become highly ironic as we venture onto the next chapter.

Chapter 9: The Grudge

New characters

- The rich man: mysterious and possibly Calvin's father

- The bishop: the superior at All Saints

This chapter delves into the one grudge that Calvin held his entire life, beginning in the Catholic boys' orphanage, All Saints.

When Calvin was ten-years-old, a rich man appeared at the home, and following his visit, the orphanage was given many educational materials like math activities and science books. Calvin discovered later that the topic of evolution was removed from the books, presumably by the orphanage, which he was punished for revealing.

Calvin had been led to believe he was orphaned, but the bishop told him that his parents, who'd died five years earlier, had adopted him. He was told that his biological mother died during birth, and his biological father couldn't handle being a single parent. The bishop implied that the rich man was Calvin's father re-entering the picture, but he was apparently uninterested in taking Calvin away with him.

Calvin's thirst for more knowledge and a connection to his mysterious father led him to study every book, fueling his fascination with science and chemistry.

A parallel can be drawn between Elizabeth and Calvin's first introduction to chemistry, which were both born from grief and mourning—from Elizabeth's brother and Calvin's guardians.

We may assume that Calvin felt abandoned once again in this flashback, as he was told by the bishop that he was unwanted and unloved. With this constant degradation and feeling of rejection, it makes the reader understand his fear of losing Elizabeth as an adult more.

Chapter 10: The Leash

New characters

- Calvin's ex-pen pal: a religious man who stopped writing back when Calvin mentioned his opinion of his father

In the present, Elizabeth heard about a new leash law for dogs and bought one for Six-thirty. She was concerned about the recent rise in the number of pets being hit by cars. She urged Calvin to use the leash when he walked Six-thirty, but he didn't like the idea because it would hinder his jogging.

Calvin mentioned that they were going to be in a rowing race the following week, drawing attention to the couple's promising future.

Being famous, he thought back to the letters he'd received through the years, which tried to convince him that they were long-lasting family members in need of money—from a supposed uncle, brother, and mother. He'd never written back, but it reminded him of an old pen pal who he'd never met but enjoyed talking to. It was only when Calvin wrote to his pen pal saying he wished his father were dead did the man stop responding.

His pen pal was the only person other than the bishop who knew of his true feelings for his father, and he felt it was already too late to reveal it to Elizabeth. Readers may note his elusive reaction when recalling his father in Chapter 5.

Elizabeth woke up early one morning and decided to go to work instead of going back to sleep. Calvin awoke an hour later, deciding to run to work with Six-thirty instead of driving because he preferred going home in one car with Elizabeth. He was still paranoid about her dying, especially in a car crash like his aunt. He chose to honor Elizabeth's wishes and took the leash with him.

The chapter ends with the shocking revelation that Calvin was dead soon after.

Chapter 11: Budget Cuts

Minutes before Calvin's death, he and Six-thirty were running past the police station like they'd done many times before. But, because of budget cuts, the police had neglected the maintenance of their cars. A loud noise from one of the badly maintained cars startled them. Six-thirty pulled on the leash in a different direction from Calvin, and as they struggled, Calvin slipped in motor oil and landed in the road. A cop car didn't see him in the early morning and drove over him.

Calvin was bleeding from the fall while Six-thirty watched helplessly from the other side of the road where he'd been thrown. The leash was broken in two, still attached to Calvin's wrist and Six-thirty's collar. This may be symbolic of the severing of their bond, as Calvin passed away shortly after.

The leash's involvement leaves questions as to what would have happened if Calvin hadn't listened to Elizabeth or if he'd simply gone to work with her. The cruel coincidence that Calvin being less stubborn by taking the leash—a sign of his character growth—played a part in his death was tragic.

The events leading up to the accident are an example of the butterfly effect. The decision to reduce the police's funding led to negligence, while the leash law led to Elizabeth's concerns and Calvin using it, and Six-thirty's past as a bomb sniffer caused his alarmed reaction.

Chapter 12: Calvin's Parting Gift

New characters

- News reporter: wrote articles that influenced public opinion

At eight years old, Elizabeth was challenged by her brother to jump into a water-filled quarry. She couldn't swim but did it anyway. She was saved by her brother then, but currently wished she'd stayed at the bottom.

Elizabeth understandably felt guilty and responsible for Calvin's death, as she'd bought the leash. She and Six-thirty fell into a deep depression, but she mustered up the strength to give the mortician his rowing clothes to be buried in, which they discarded and dressed him in a suit anyway.

Rowers and employees from Hastings attended the funeral, extending their condolences, despite them secretly cheering because they were jealous of Calvin.

Elizabeth's depression had manifested into suicidal thoughts, which Six-thirty also shared. However, the dog and the woman cared so much for each other that they were willing to go on for the other's sake.

They were standing far away from the funeral, which a nearby reporter took as an invitation to ask her about Calvin and his love life, family, and flaws. He took her unresponsiveness and emotionless state as her being blind and tried to lead her to the crowd but was shocked when she pulled away. He pressed on about a rumor that Calvin was "a jerk" (Garmus, 2022, p. 100), and when she denied it, he thought it to be because *she* was misunderstanding him and not the other way around.

His tone was condescending and callous as he made horrible remarks about Calvin while still not knowing that Elizabeth was his partner. This may be an example of the casual misogyny of the time: assuming she's strange or asking for his help by simply existing.

Elizabeth and Six-thirty walked home after the funeral and saw the blossoming flowers announcing the coming of Spring. The contrast of Elizabeth being at her lowest point during Spring—symbolic of new beginnings and hope—creates irony but may also hint at something new on the way.

It was too hard to be at home without Calvin, so they went to work. Elizabeth's colleagues were uncomfortable around her broken state and avoided her. She and Six-thirty entered Calvin's lab to see all of his things packed in boxes, ready to be fetched by a blood relative. Since Elizabeth and Calvin weren't married, she wasn't legally allowed to look at or take anything. Miss Frask, the secretary from Chapter 6, informed her of this and that Six-thirty wouldn't be allowed at work anymore since it was leniency on Calvin's account. Unbeknownst to Frask, Elizabeth had already taken the ring that Calvin had proposed to her with.

Miss Frask implied that Elizabeth *rode his coattails*, meaning to benefit from someone else's success and use it to your own advantage. She further implied that Elizabeth and Calvin's relationship was shallow, meaningless, and easily replaceable.

Frask detested Elizabeth because of her attractiveness and disregard for tradition and said she should stop pursuing chemistry to have many children. She then instructed Elizabeth to take more time off right before Elizabeth threw up in the sink.

Frask showed Elizabeth a newspaper article by the reporter at the funeral which suggested that Calvin's unlikable nature affected his career and that his own partner barely knew him. Elizabeth threw up again.

After the vomiting, Frask realized something that Elizabeth didn't until now: she was pregnant.

There was an immense lack of human empathy in this chapter, from colleagues rejoicing in Calvin's death to Frask's treatment of Elizabeth. As readers, we understand the truth of the situation, but to outsiders, Elizabeth and Calvin's happiness was unfair. *How dare they find true love while everyone else was miserable?*

It goes to show that jealousy and greed stem from people's self-hatred and unhappiness with their own lives. The status quo of the '60s meant that people put what society deemed correct before their own happiness, resulting in feelings of unfulfillment, which they took out on others.

The horrible effects of closed-minded views and ignorance are an important theme, with this chapter being an example.

Chapter 13: Idiots

The chapter begins from the point of view of the personified Hastings Management and their cold-hearted corporate approach to getting funding by any means necessary.

In a time-jump to the events of Chapter 8, it's revealed how Calvin further pushed to get abiogenesis the funding it deserved, stating that Elizabeth's "ideas might even be better than his own" (Garmus, 2022, p. 110).

Back to the present, the news article had left a bad impression of Calvin, which affected Hastings as the investors started questioning their financial backing. However, a mysterious rich sponsor with an interest in abiogenesis appeared just in time.

Having misrepresented Elizabeth as a man, Hastings conveniently prevented the man from meeting the woman he was funding by making her unavailable. If it came to light that the chemist was an unmarried pregnant woman, Hastings would be ruined. Also, thanks to Miss Frask's gossiping, everyone now knew of Elizabeth's pregnancy.

Hastings planned to replace her with one of the other three chemists she'd been working with, but as it happens, she was the only competent one who did all the work. Dr. Boryweitz had even tried to take the credit but was quickly found out.

Miss Frask and Dr. Donatti were to fire Elizabeth as soon as possible. They refused to state the reason, and when Elizabeth matter-of-factly suggested her pregnancy as the cause, they were stunned. It was normal for the women to be held responsible in these situations while the man remained unaffected. Donatti was offended that Elizabeth, a woman, was explaining pregnancy to him. To further the irony and entitlement of this, he insisted that the reason was legitimate, despite Elizabeth knowing that it wasn't in the employee handbook.

They ushered her out, and Donatti offhandedly mentioned how Calvin had demanded that they fund her project. Elizabeth was shocked by this new information. Her trust had been broken, and her life was crumbling around her.

Chapter 14: Grief

Calvin's gravestone had been made, but the engraved quote was cut off due to a lack of planning and read, "Your days are numbered" (Garmus, 2022, p. 116). The ominous statement reflected Elizabeth's current feelings, amplified by Calvin's sudden death: time was invaluable, and life was short.

Elizabeth was teaching Six-thirty words using a children's educational technique; she read through picture books with him to teach image association.

Six-thirty used these words to communicate with others in his mind and would try to talk with the baby inside of Elizabeth's stomach. On his visits to Calvin's grave, which the cemetery's groundskeeper wouldn't allow, he expressed his worries over Elizabeth's mental state. She'd torn down the kitchen a few months earlier to make room for a home laboratory. With some do-it-yourself skills and salvaging, she created makeshift appliances. The result was an impressively functional and advanced lab.

After Elizabeth was fired, it was obvious that Hastings's chemists were lost without her, as many showed up asking for help. She realized the potential for income and started charging for her time, completing their work for them just as she'd done when she was employed.

Six-thirty's concerns only grew as Elizabeth overworked herself and neglected her health. While communicating with Calvin on one visit, the groundskeeper found Six-thirty and shot at him. Six-thirty knocked him down, injuring him, and was about to bite but instead barked to get help. Six-thirty understood compassion better than most of the humans.

The news reporter from the funeral returned Six-thirty home safely and assured Elizabeth that he'd write a story that painted Six-thirty as a hero. He did, and it resulted in the groundskeeper being fired.

In the article's picture, Elizabeth could see Calvin's gravestone, which was shot by the groundskeeper. It now read, "Your days are nu" (Garmus, 2022, p. 124)—said out loud as "Your days are new." This is the same saying that Calvin used to tell his younger self, first mentioned in Chapter 5. This coincidence may be a way of Calvin motivating Elizabeth even after death, in the same way, he used to do for himself. Every day is new, and with it comes new challenges but also new beginnings.

Chapter 15: Unsolicited Advice

Navigating day-to-day life as a pregnant woman invited many unwelcome remarks from strangers. Many sought to remind Elizabeth that anything she was feeling was about to get worse, and others felt the need to tell her what gender *they* thought the baby would be.

After the incident with the groundskeeper, Elizabeth had a new gravestone for Calvin made, now engraved with a complicated formula of the "chemical response" that created "happiness" (Garmus, 2022, p. 127). No one else understood it but her, further unifying the love and bond between them.

Elizabeth made an appointment for a check-up with Dr. Mason, the coxswain. In the elevator on her way to the office, a man tapped her stomach like a drum without consent, and she responded with a purse to the groin.

To Dr. Mason's surprise, Elizabeth said she'd been erging. He admitted that it'll help her in preparation for labor, but he couldn't understand why she willingly put herself through the pain. He asked why she waited so late to come in, and she lied, blaming work.

The truth was that she secretly hoped that she would lose the baby, which would explain her overexertion while erging and the delay of her first check-up.

Dr. Mason finished the examination and acknowledged the hardships that she was enduring. For the first time in her life, someone recognized her struggle, and she started to tear up.

Mason cautiously explained that he wasn't judgmental and that he understood her conflict. He believed that women shouldn't be compelled to bring children into the world unwillingly. He asked if she had anyone to help her with the baby, and she could only think of her dog.

Mason didn't seem phased by this answer and urged her to row again as soon as she could, offering her a seat on his boat.

He was the first person since Calvin to treat her normally and not question or judge her for being unmarried to Calvin or why she insisted on being called Miss Zott and not Mrs. Evans. This compassion was her glimmer of hope—her new day—that assured her that she wasn't alone or horrible for feeling the way she did.

Chapter 16: Labor

Several weeks later, Elizabeth was about to borrow some new books for Six-thirty, as he was rapidly progressing with his word learning. While walking to the library, Elizabeth felt what she thought were hunger pains. She'd been monitoring herself and estimated her due date, but she was unknowingly in labor at that moment.

13 hours later, Dr. Mason delivered a baby girl and observed that she'll be a rower. The next day, Elizabeth checked herself out despite being urged to stay in recovery for a few more days, with the excuse that she was going to erg.

When they got home, Elizabeth introduced the baby to Six-thirty, who mistook her name as Nine Twenty-two after the time they had arrived.

This was very similar to how Six-thirty had been accepted into the family. Small steps on the path to healing can be seen here, as Elizabeth and Six-thirty felt happiness for the first time in months—as a family of three again.

Chapter 17: Harriet Sloane

New characters

- Harriet Sloane: Elizabeth's wise older neighbor

Elizabeth struggled with the challenges of being a new mother, such as meal preparation, changing diapers, burping, cleaning, and so on. Elizabeth was governed by reason and logic and was dumbfounded by her infant daughter's ever-changing needs and inability to follow the schedule she'd set for her.

Another reason she declined anesthesia during labor was her finances; her new business of doing ex-colleagues' work for money wasn't enough to support a child.

Dr. Boryweitz appeared one morning, desperate for Elizabeth's help, as he had a meeting with Donatti, but after she helped him and went to do her own work, she collapsed in exhaustion.

Elizabeth dreamed of Calvin and her reading a book. While reading, she noted that fiction was troublesome. She said that there's no way to be sure how the author meant for the story to be interpreted—possible dramatic irony and fourth wall break.

Harriet Sloane, Elizabeth's neighbor, found her asleep on the floor. After making sure that Elizabeth was alright, she changed the baby. This was the first mention of the baby's name: Madeline.

Harriet was shocked by Elizabeth's lab where a kitchen should be and more so by her scientific method of making coffee. Harriet recognized the book about childcare that Elizabeth had bought and commented how ironic it was that a man had written a book about labor and childcare. She hypothesized that his wife had written it, and he'd taken the credit, which both Elizabeth and Harriet agreed on.

Harriet was an experienced mother of four and said things as they were, calling babies "horrible", a "devil", and a "gremlin" (Garmus, 2022, p. 142-145). She told Elizabeth the harsh reality of motherhood: there are hardly any of the joyous moments that magazines describe, and it's normal to want to give your baby away during the hardships. Harriet left with a piece of advice that she herself wasn't able to follow: Take a moment every day to tend to your own needs. She gave Elizabeth a home-baked casserole and told her to call her anytime.

This seemed to be the only way Elizabeth could accept help: forcefully. Harriet was going to give her help whether she liked it or not, and Elizabeth was admittedly grateful.

Chapter 18: Legally Mad

New characters

- Mr. Sloane: Harriet's chauvinistic husband

At the beginning of Calvin and Elizabeth's relationship, Harriet, like everyone, thought their relationship was shallow and based on Elizabeth's looks, but as she watched their daily life together, she started to see them as soulmates.

Unlike them, Harriet wasn't in love with her husband at all. He made vulgar comments about Elizabeth, openly pleasured himself next to Harriet, and was shameless about his lust for other women. While Harriet thought of herself as unattractive, she considered Mr. Sloane ugly, inside and out.

Harriet intently watched Elizabeth's house from across the street after Calvin died and saw all the men that visited. She realized she was being just as judgmental as Mr. Sloane and decided to visit, finding Elizabeth on the floor in Chapter 17.

Afterward, Harriet secretly begged for Elizabeth to call.

Elizabeth recalled the events of childbirth; while screaming in pain, she'd accidentally dug into a nurse's arm. The same nurse came to ask how she was doing after. Truthfully, Elizabeth was furious at Calvin for lying and pushing funding for her research and for his easily preventable death. So, she told the nurse that she was mad. The nurse, likely still sensitive over her arm, wrote "Mad" on the paper.

The paper was the birth certificate, meaning the baby's name was now "legally Mad" (Garmus, 2022, p. 154). Elizabeth hadn't thought of a name prior and hoped it would come to her when she saw her baby, but it hadn't. She went to legally change the name, but it required personal details like a marriage certificate. She tried several other names before realizing that "Mad" had stuck.

The chapter ends with Elizabeth finally giving in and calling Harriet, showing her character development.

Chapter 19: December 1956

A year later, Madeline was learning how to speak and repeat words. Six-thirty acted as her protector, determined to never let another loved one be hurt again.

Elizabeth's mothering method was unusual, calling it "experimental learning" (Garmus, 2022, p. 157) as she encouraged Madeline to explore and discover things, however dangerous.

Dr. Mason arrived to check in, as he said he would when Madeline was born. He asked about parenting, erging, and if anyone was helping her. While talking, he started doing the dishes and folding diapers and mentioned the open seat he still had on his rows. She made the excuse that she was busy, and he replied that they row early in the morning, so it'll be fine.

While Elizabeth knew she and Calvin talked about not having children, she was grieving the great father he would've been. As a single mother, she constantly felt like she was failing some kind of parenting test, but it was clear that Madeline and Elizabeth were learning from each other. Elizabeth was awestruck at how Madeline could find wonder in even the most mundane things.

Dr. Mason expressed again that Madeline will be a rower. He also noticed that she could read a person by their body language. He talked of a new rowing coach and how he'd mentioned Elizabeth to him, failing to say if the coach knew she was a woman.

Both he and Calvin prioritized rowing over everything else. Mason motivated her to ask Harriet to babysit at 4:30 a.m. when they would row. To her surprise, Harriet accepted because she wanted to get away from Mr. Sloane.

The rowers and coach seemed displeased at her arrival on the day. After the row, Mason assured her that everything went well, even though she thought otherwise. He would use euphemisms to downplay everything, like when she had an excruciating contraction during labor, and he said it wasn't "so bad" (Garmus, 2022, p. 165).

Despite the exhaustion, she was relieved to be rowing again. Mason compared rowing to raising children: both required resilience and perseverance, and you could only see your past actions and never where you're headed.

Chapter 20: Life Story

New characters

- Mrs. Mudford: Madeline's conservative teacher

Madeline was nearly four and rapidly progressing in height and reading ability, but she struggled to interact with people similar to her mother and was lacking in normal skills like tying shoelaces. To expose her to kids her age, Elizabeth signed her up for kindergarten. Madeline was still a year too young, so Elizabeth changed her birth certificate so she could be accepted.

Harriet felt good being needed and didn't want Madeline to go. Similarly, Six-thirty was worried about Madeline not being under his protection at school.

Madeline made a chalk drawing of what she called her "life story" (Garmus, 2022, p. 170), which had pictures of her mom rowing, the sun, moon, flowers, Six-thirty, and more. In the middle was a spiral named "the pit of death" (Garmus, 2022, p. 170), surrounded by tears. As Mason had said, Elizabeth could read a person, and the sadness in her drawing represented her mom's unhappiness.

Ultimately, sending Madeline to school was also a way for Elizabeth to find time to get a job. They were struggling, and she'd already borrowed money with a reversal of their mortgage. She discovered that, thankfully, Calvin had added her name to the house's deed, so they didn't have to depend on a social grant to get by.

Their situation meant she had to ignore Harriet's warnings and unwillingly ask for a job back at Hastings.

Donatti was happy that Calvin and Elizabeth were gone, but nothing was being done on abiogenesis, which agitated the mysterious investor. He couldn't afford to employ Elizabeth again, but he also couldn't afford to lose the funding from the man. Boryweitz seemed to have made progress, but it was revealed all his findings were from talking to Elizabeth.

Employing her was his only option.

Chapter 21: E.Z.

Hastings welcomed Elizabeth back with a new lab coat embroidered with "E.Z." instead of "E. Zott" like her old one. It purposefully sounded like "easy," which was used to crudely describe a woman who was supposedly easy to sleep with.

Donatti mentioned that he knew Elizabeth was still pursuing abiogenesis, which only Dr. Boryweitz knew, as she'd caught him going through her files once during a visit. Donatti added that he'd written a paper about an unexciting topic that'll be published soon.

He told her she wouldn't be getting her old job or salary back and that she'd start as a lab technician. Stating that she wouldn't get the so-called special treatment she'd received before, he called her the demeaning "Luscious" (Garmus, 2022, p. 174). Before she can react, he said they'll pay for her advanced education, casually adding that it's actually an at-home typewriting course.

Furious, Elizabeth stormed into the bathroom and into a stall next to Miss Frask. It's revealed to the reader that Frask still hadn't been promoted in four years and was now answering to an inexperienced college boy who'd instructed her to lose weight.

They engaged in a bitter conversation, where Frask snidely apologized for Elizabeth having a daughter instead of a son. At daycare, Madeline had wanted something in blue instead of pink, which was met with disapproval from her teacher, Mrs. Mudford.

Miss Frask unknowingly revealed to Elizabeth the origin of abiogenesis's funding—the rich sponsor. She implied that the donor and she were romantically involved and divulged that Elizabeth was being misrepresented to him as a man.

They argued, and Elizabeth found out that Miss Frask was an "*almost*-psychologist" (Garmus, 2022, p. 178), leading to them admitting that they were both sexually assaulted by their advisors and were never able to complete their PHDs.

Chapter 22: The Present

At Hastings, Elizabeth, and Miss Frask unknowingly started to bond. Elizabeth asked her to find out more about the sponsor, but Frask couldn't find anything. Frask matter-of-factly told Elizabeth over lunch that she'd been fired because she gained weight instead of losing it. Elizabeth urged her to fight against the unfair and illegal dismissal, but Frask expressed that there wasn't a way and that she already had typewriting job opportunities.

Frask apparently had a gift for Elizabeth, which was Calvin's old belongings that no one had claimed from Chapter 12. It was illegal, but neither one cared as they took out the boxes.

Two women wronged by Hastings, their university advisors, and society—they had a lot more in common than they thought.

Chapter 23: KCTV Studios

New and revised characters

- Mr. Wakely: Calvin's religious, surfer ex-pen pal

- Tommy Dixon: Madeline's classmate who thinks her family is poor

After being employed for two months, Elizabeth was immensely overqualified and bored by her underpaying job. That month, Donatti's paper was published, which was completely plagiarized from her own work. The day she'd been reemployed, Donatti photocopied her documents, which Boryweitz had seen and done nothing about.

Donatti published it to please the investor, who was disappointed by "Mr. Zott's" lack of performance, not knowing that she'd been fired years ago.

Elizabeth stormed into Donatti's office to confront him while he hardly paid attention. But what he couldn't have her do, because of his promises to the investor, was quit, which she did right then and there.

Elizabeth arrived home and was greeted by Harriet and her daughter. The arrangement was that Harriet dropped Madeline off at kindergarten, Six-thirty fetched her, and Harriet babysat her until Elizabeth returned.

Madeline was unhappy that her classmates didn't like her show-and-tell objects, which ranged from sailing knots to the head of an arrow. She would tie the knots outside in rainstorms as if she was preparing for doomsday. Her father's death left her with the feeling that she needed to be prepared for something bad.

Elizabeth had many talks with Madeline's teacher because Madeline apparently asked "inappropriate questions" (Garmus, 2022, p. 188). Ironically, Madeline asked at dinner if they didn't have money since that's what Tommy Dixon, a boy at school, said.

Prompted by this, Elizabeth thought back to what she found in one of the boxes she took from Hastings, called "Rowing." Inside were all of Calvin's employment offers, many of which were higher paying than Hastings. She then found the letters from all the fake family members but noted one particular "mother" who wanted to give money for his research instead of taking it.

In a file called "Wakely," she found letters from his ex-pen pal from around ten years ago. Mr. Wakely was a religious surfer and wrote to Calvin about the simultaneous existence of both science and God. Calvin refused the notion, and they debated back and forth. In one letter, Wakely mentioned that Commons's weather was great. Elizabeth deduced that Calvin chose to work in Commons because of the optimal rowing weather.

Calvin seemed to have convinced Wakely that religion wasn't that different from believing in fairy tales, which had simpler morals. Wakely mentioned he'd come from a lineage of ministers and asked about Calvin's father, to which Calvin replied in all capitals, saying he hated his father and hoped he was dead. Elizabeth was shocked. She thought his father was already dead from a train accident, as she'd been told by him in Chapter 5.

In the present, TV producer Walter Pine was struggling to find a show to fill the empty afternoon slot, which his job depended on. He'd been confronted by Elizabeth days before because of his daughter's lunch theft. He was divorced, and because he was tired and stressed, Amanda often went to school with mistakenly packed alcohol or objects in her lunchbox, explaining the lunch theft.

After the encounter, he couldn't stop thinking about Elizabeth, and after many missed calls, he finally reached her when Madeline answered. He spoke to Elizabeth about the prospects of a cooking show produced by KCTV, which she would host. She'd start immediately and be paid well. Despite her reservations, she accepted.

Chapter 24: The Afternoon Depression Zone

New characters

- Phil Lebensmal: Walter Pine's demanding and crude boss

At the fitting of Elizabeth's wardrobe, she was very displeased at the tight outfits which were demanded by Phil Lebensmal, Walter's boss. Phil wanted Elizabeth to portray an objectified and sexualized housewife that appealed to men's idea of the so-called perfect woman, also wanting her to make a cocktail at the end of every episode. Walter tried to oppose this but was pressurized because Phil was his boss.

Elizabeth was adamant that she wouldn't wear the dresses and suggested that they compromise by her wearing a lab coat. Walter denied it, thinking of Phil's demands. Elizabeth's scientific approach to everything perplexed him, as she'd wanted to do a trial run with the lab coat and assess the results.

The TV set was a *typical* stay-at-home wife's kitchen approved by Walter that he knew Elizabeth would despise. Elizabeth wanted the exact opposite and requested chemistry-related revisions and appliances like Bunsen burners and a steel countertop.

Elizabeth stated that cooking wasn't "fun" (Garmus, 2022, p. 204), to which Walter explained the Afternoon Depression Zone concept: between 1 p.m. and 5 p.m., humans were at their least productive and most half-asleep. Except for housewives, who were expected to get everything done quickly before dinner. Walter offered the solution as afternoon TV, which was brain-numbing enough to rest the mind and wake people up. He stressed the importance of being entertaining because the show aired at 4:30 p.m., nearing the end of the Zone as dinner preparation started.

Walter used a dinner party as an example of fun and assumed that she and "Mr. Zott" would hold them. Elizabeth corrected him by saying she wasn't married, and when he supposed it to be an affair, she explained it was because she didn't want marriage. He advised her to not tell anyone else because it was frowned upon. She told him Calvin died, and Walter saw her grief and consoled her.

She mentioned his dissolved marriage, which he explained wasn't based on love anyway. He'd also recently discovered that he wasn't Amanda's biological father, which didn't matter to him.

They bonded over them both having to constantly meet Mrs. Mudford, who'd convinced herself that Walter was a pedophile because he was a single father.

Walter was surprised at how open and honest they were with each other, more so than he'd ever been with anyone. An unlikely friendship began forming.

Elizabeth insisted that she won't pretend to be something she was not to appease Phil; she was, first and foremost, a scientist.

Unknown to Walter, this unapologetic personality won't be her downfall but will instead be what makes her a star.

Chapter 25: The Average Jane

New characters

- Rosa: Elizabeth's hair and make-up stylist

The first airing of the show didn't go to plan. Elizabeth had practiced reading from the cue cards, and Walter instructed her to just do as she was told—which wasn't known to be Elizabeth's style.

She walked onto the stage and ignored the prompts to start the show and instead looked around the set for the first time. It looked like the stereotypical housewife kitchen, with a fake window and props like sewing items, a cookie jar, and a Jesus statuette. She said it was dreadful and spoke directly to Walter while live.

Commercials rolled to prevent further damage, and Walter shouted at her to follow the script. She instructed that the set had to be changed, but he said it was tailored to what the "average" woman wanted. She asserted that she was a woman and hated it.

After the break, she read the cue cards but stopped at the word "fun" (Garmus, 2022, p. 216). A moment passed, but she suddenly recovered and went off script. As she removed the silly props from her workspace, she stated that she meant business and knew the struggles of being a wife and mother. Somewhere, a housewife unintentionally heard this on the TV and stopped to listen.

Once the show ended, Elizabeth's stylist, Rosa, tried complimenting the pencil in Elizabeth's hair to ease the tension while Walter was being lectured by Phil. Elizabeth was satisfied with the episode, but Phil wasn't.

Walter scolded her, but she said she couldn't read the cards, actually meaning she had too much pride to read them.

An assistant interrupted to say that they were getting calls about the show to ask about an ingredient that was given in chemical form. Elizabeth explained it was vinegar; she had the idea during filming to give the audience a list of groceries for the next episode.

Even though Walter was furious at how Elizabeth changed things at her whim, he realized he'd never received phone calls for any of his previous shows.

Chapter 26: The Funeral

After a constant back-and-forth between Walter and Elizabeth, he decided to make her do an episode with live viewers in the hopes she'd follow the script under pressure.

But the first thing she did was hand out all the set's props to the audience, throwing some for the viewers to catch. She improvised, detailing the elemental makeup of spinach as Walter tried to calm down.

During a commercial break, she excitedly explained that she'd tried to engage the live viewers by using sports stadium tactics: throwing things into the crowd. He wasn't amused.

She went back to the stage, and he envisioned his own funeral, willing for death. The attendants were dressed in bright colors, and some told the boring story of his death. Elizabeth was reading his eulogy, which was absurdly motivational and inspiring. He was brought back to reality by Elizabeth's show-ending quote: "Children, set the table. Your mother needs a moment to herself" (Garmus, 2022, p. 226), which was inspired by the advice Harriet gave her in Chapter 17.

Walter had fainted because of the stress and from not eating and was awoken by Rosa and Elizabeth. Elizabeth offered the dish she'd made on the show. He declined, saying his daughter disliked spinach, but Elizabeth left it for him in his car anyway. He was so exhausted that he ended up taking it home. When they dug in, Amanda said it was the most delicious thing she'd ever eaten.

Chapter 27: All About Me

It was May 1960, and Madeline's class was tasked to do a family tree assignment to learn more about themselves. As Mrs. Mudford was trying to get them to guess that it was about themselves, she argued with Madeline, who said humans were animals. This caused the class to erupt into chaos. Mudford threatened to call the principal, which restored order. When it was home time, she made Madeline stay late because of her "humans are animals" comment.

At home, Harriet tried to explain to Madeline that sometimes she had to politely agree with someone even if they were wrong. Madeline couldn't understand this like when Mudford said that everything was made by God, and Madeline didn't believe her. Madeline asked if Harriet was a believer in God, which Harriet was, as Harriet believed it was a requirement in life. She also wanted hell to be real so that Mr. Sloane would end up there.

Madeline showed Harriet the family tree, and Harriet expressed that it was problematic because it made you establish your identity in relation to someone else. Harriet told her not to show it to Elizabeth, but Madeline didn't know much about her father, and she needed a photo of the whole family with him in it. She'd tried to find his university's yearbooks, but the librarian disregarded her request.

Harriet listed Calvin's family members and accidentally mentioned his "godmother" (Garmus, 2022, p. 232). She knew of this so-called godmother because she'd poked around his house prior to him meeting Elizabeth when he'd left his front door open in a rush. She went to shut it but then started to look around, finding a request for funding from his old boys' home, which he'd chucked away.

Currently, Harriet explained to Madeline that a godmother was a friend or family member that helped maintain a child's religion. She'd actually meant the expression "fairy godmother," referring to the rich man who'd sponsored All Saints. She advised Madeline against adding him to her family tree as most donors preferred to be private, which Madeline thought meant having secrets. Madeline asked Harriet if she'd ever kept secrets, and Harriet lied and said no.

Harriet was dumbfounded by Madeline's odd interests and pastimes, like reading complex literature and researching natural disasters. Harriett accredited Madeline's extraordinary abilities to Elizabeth, who'd pushed her young daughter to learn to read. Elizabeth had also found a way to make cooking both serious and motivational, with even Harriet learning more about chemistry during her show.

Supper at Six's six-month trial was almost up, and Elizabeth thought it'd be canceled, but Madeline said to Harriet that some kids at school got a lunch similar to hers, meaning their parents watched the show.

Because of the show, Elizabeth was able to pay Harriet for babysitting. Though, Elizabeth still wouldn't compromise her beliefs, even when Harriet urged her to pander to Phil to keep the job.

Harriet believed men required special treatment because of their "fragile egos" (Garmus, 2022, p. 237), while Elizabeth treated them as she wished she was treated—as equals.

Elizabeth went to talk with Mrs. Mudford about Madeline not wanting to do stereotypical girl activities. Madeline wanted to go on "safety patrol" (Garmus, 2022, p. 238), which was reserved for boys, according to Mudford. Madeline was also the tallest in the class, which hurt the boys' feelings.

This furthered Elizabeth's position of never diminishing herself or her talents to make men feel better, but when she expressed this to Harriet, Harriet said nothing.

Religion was explored from both sides—Harriet's faith that she felt required to uphold and Madeline and Elizabeth's atheism. Similarly, the themes of gender norms are explored, with Madeline representing its enforcement on young impressionable minds and Elizabeth representing its undoing by teaching women that they aren't limited or defined by their gender.

Chapter 28: Saints

Revised characters

- Reverend Wakely: a not-so-religious minister who was Calvin's pen pal

Madeline went to the city's library to discover more about the boys' home where her father grew up. She knew the address was in Iowa and that the name sounded "girlish" (Garmus, 2022, p. 232), according to Harriet.

A minister overheard Madeline and the librarian and interrupted to offer suggestions. According to him, religious orphanages were often named after different saints because people who raised children were saints themselves since childcare was difficult. He learned that Madeline was making a family tree, and he had similar views to Harriet on it: you can't define yourself by your ancestry.

Madeline thought the orphanage staff would be the closest thing to family for her father, but the minister considered that, with what he'd experienced, many were pedophiles.

He came to realize that his job was a paradox as he regularly lied to reassure people better days would come even when he knew they wouldn't.

Throughout their interaction, the minister treated her as an adult and didn't talk down to her and was also the only person who exclusively called her "Mad" and not "Madeline." He truthfully admitted that he had secrets like everyone else, contrasting her earlier conversation with Harriet.

He introduced himself as Wakely, and Madeline was able to find the orphanage's name thanks to his help. There was just a contact number listed, but she couldn't involve her mother or make long-distance phone calls. Wakely offered to call them for her and was shocked when she said her father was Calvin Evans, his old pen pal.

When Wakely was a Harvard student, he took a course on chemistry in an effort to prove that God created everything and discredit those who thought otherwise. But he ended up disproving his own beliefs, which was troublesome as he was studying religion.

One night he went to watch a panel of researchers which included Calvin Evans. Calvin didn't say anything except to mention religion as an example of something that was unchanging and impactful but lacked energy. This prompted Wakely to write to Calvin, starting their pen pal correspondence.

Although they debated God and science, they progressed to more personal topics, but when the subject of fathers arose, and Calvin replied aggressively, Wakely didn't know how to respond, so they never spoke again.

Wakely graduated, and his father passed soon after in Commons. Wakely stayed in the Commons and took his father's place in the ministry. He eventually learned

Calvin lived in the same town, but Calvin died before they could meet in person. To pay respects, Wakely volunteered to officiate his funeral.

He'd seen Elizabeth and Six-thirty at the funeral but never found the right time to introduce himself, but as fate would have it, Calvin's daughter was now in front of him.

Madeline found the picture from the article about Calvin's funeral, containing her mom and Six-thirty. She took it as her family photo because Elizabeth was pregnant in it, so Madeline was technically in the photo.

Before Madeline left, she asked Wakely if he could keep a secret. She shared a secret with him, and he shared something with her, both unknown to the reader.

By withholding information about Calvin's past while he was alive, the readers are able to experience and gradually discover information as Madeline does. This creates a visceral experience as we learn how detached Madeline feels from Calvin and how she desperately needs more information to feel connected to him, similar to the connection he felt for his biological father, albeit under different circumstances.

Chapter 29: Bonding

In another episode of *Supper at Six*, Elizabeth was explaining the different kinds of chemical bonds. She used easy-to-understand metaphors by comparing them to marriages. People in the audience and at home took notes of everything she said.

She likened ionic bonds to the concept of *opposites attract*, like the marriage of two completely different people who were still strongly connected. The covalent bond was compared to two people using their strengths to make something better, like bringing food and wine to a dinner party. The hydrogen bond was equated to *love at first sight*, which was powerful but easily broken, like finding out something unpleasant about your partner in a new relationship.

Because of this, a mother used her new chemical knowledge to appeal to her daughter to further her education and not be hindered by her boyfriend. This showed that Elizabeth had planted the seeds of change, making women across America rethink their daughters' and their own roles in society.

On the other hand, Walter was only able to extend the show's running time if Elizabeth did what Phil wanted. People were complaining about the show due to Elizabeth's unorthodox teachings, but Elizabeth rejected any of Walter's requests for changes.

Walter disliked Elizabeth's use of scientific diction, but it made Rosa and the women watching feel powerful and "capable" (Garmus, 2022, p. 255). Rosa's use of the scientific word for aspirin and the fact that Elizabeth was wearing pants irritated Walter.

He wasn't only perpetually stressed over the show, he was also worried over Amanda's family tree project. It stressed the importance of biological bonds, which he and she didn't have, and required a picture with her mother, who was no longer in her life.

Walter ignored Elizabeth when she tried to ask for fire extinguishers for the chemistry lesson in the next episode.

Elizabeth finished the chicken pot pie she was making, comparing its mixture of ingredients to a well-operating society like Sweden. She asked the live crowd for any questions, much to the cameraman's dismay. A woman stood up and revealed that she'd always wanted to be an open-heart surgeon but couldn't because of her circumstances. Elizabeth encouraged her to pursue her dreams even while being a mother of four. The crowd applauded her, and Elizabeth gave her the chicken pot pie to take home as a part of "Free Day"—a way to give away more things that she gave credit to Walter for creating.

Alongside chemistry, Elizabeth instilled the ideas of subsidizing childcare and moving to Sweden for a better quality of life in her audience. She challenged the status quo and empowered and taught women that they *are* smart enough for anything, despite what they'd been told.

Chapter 30: 99 Percent

Madeline had turned in her assignment with the newspaper picture and a family tree full of famous historical figures, with the addition of an acorn as the "fairy godmother"—All Saints's sponsor. She'd also written on it that humans were ninety-nine percent identical (Garmus, 2022, p. 262). Instead of lecturing Madeline on the other matters, Elizabeth tried explaining the concept of decimals so that Madeline could be more accurate in her percentage.

Harriet gave Elizabeth a list of phone messages left for her. One was from Wakely, which she disregarded, and the other from *LA Times*, a magazine. The latter had asked for an interview, which Elizabeth declined as they'd only wanted to discuss cooking and not chemistry.

Madeline asked if something was wrong with their family and for more information on her dad. Elizabeth replied that nothing was wrong and that she'd already told her everything about Calvin. Elizabeth suspected Calvin was private about his time in the boys' home because of his trauma, and Madeline asked if something bad had happened to her too, but she didn't hear her.

Walter called Elizabeth to talk about Mrs. Mudford, who wasn't happy with his daughter's project, similar to Madeline's. Next year, Mrs. Mudford would be Madeline's teacher again, and Elizabeth wanted to complain. Walter mentioned Phil was unhappy, and

Elizabeth wanted to lodge a complaint about him too. Walter asked her to incorporate the use of a brand of soup in the show so that they'd be sponsored and maybe left alone by Phil.

The next day the results of the family tree assignment spread like wildfire, with Madeline's parents being unmarried, Tommy's father an alcohol addict, and Amanda not having a mom. Mudford used all of this to gossip to the mothers.

A day later, Elizabeth found out that she was paid significantly lower than her male colleagues. She'd also discovered that Harriet had been physically abused by Mr. Sloane. Elizabeth wanted to involve the police, but Harriet reminded her that they'd do nothing and only blame her if she injured him.

Later on the show, Elizabeth tossed the canned soup Walter asked her to use in the garbage and seriously explained the different kinds of deadly mushrooms, which could be used to inconspicuously poison someone while people made notes. Once the show ended, Rosa informed her that Phil wanted to talk alone, but Rosa was worried and wanted her to tell Walter, who'd left early. Elizabeth said it'd be fine.

In Phil's office, he chastised her about the show's complaints and apparent bad ratings. He threatened her job, and when she didn't react as he hoped, he fired her and everyone on the show. He tried to intimidate and command authority, which was met with no emotional response from Elizabeth.

She explained that he wanted a show that enforced "societal norms" (Garmus, 2022, p. 274), and she wanted to encourage people to think logically and feel like they belong, even while living in a society that devalued differences. She added that Walter wasn't at fault and that he'd tried to get her to do what Phil wanted.

Phil had taken ten alkalizer tablets in the two hours prior and smoked a cigarette before downing two shots of whiskey. He was furious and about to try to sexually assault her, but suddenly fainted just as she'd calmly taken out a long sharp knife to defend herself with.

Chapter 31: The Get-Well Card

Phil was hospitalized after a heart attack. Elizabeth had called the ambulance, and Walter was desperate to know what happened that night. He never wanted anyone to meet with Phil alone, as he knew he was a bad man, but he also knew he'd never done anything *about* men like Phil.

She told him that he'd fired her, him, and everyone on the show and that he said that Walter had "failed to rein [her] in" (Garmus, 2022, p. 279). Walter defended himself, saying he'd never forced her to wear the tight dresses or read the cue cards, even though he wished she would since he wrote them. He explained that he tried to get on Phil's good side and do what he asked because that's how things got done.

The truth was that the show had more viewer interaction, like fan mail and calls, than any other show, despite Phil telling him that their sponsors were about to leave and that the audience disliked her.

Walter was distraught when she revealed the events of that night and that Phil had tried to assault her.

When she'd called the ambulance, she looked through Phil's office and found many advertisements and sponsorship offers, which she showed Walter. Some involved syndication, which would mean airing the show on other television stations outside of Commons.

A few days later, Walter took over Phil's job. Elizabeth advised him to do the right thing now that he was in a position of power, even if he had to pretend. So, he did and secured many sponsorship deals and told everyone that Elizabeth had saved Phil's life.

He had a Get-Well-Soon card made that had a drawing of Phil holding his heart like a football. Inside, people wrote well-wishes but also messages that conveyed their true feelings—swearing and cursing him. A secretary's message that wished Phil death and Rosa's comforting reaction to Elizabeth days after the incident could imply that it wasn't the first time he'd assaulted someone.

After years of following Phil's orders and doing nothing about his disgusting ways, Walter finally took action and vowed to make changes, writing in the card that he hoped Phil never recovered.

Chapter 32: Medium Rare

New characters

- Seymour Browne: parking attendant at KCTV

Mrs. Mudford was Madeline's teacher again at the start of the next school year, and because of this, Harriet allowed—and encouraged—Madeline to skip school, which she knew Elizabeth wouldn't approve of. Harriet forged a note, and the two went on their way to see *Supper at Six* live. But when they arrived, there were hundreds of people waiting in line with the exact same idea. The parking attendant stopped them as there was no more parking space.

He tried to turn them away and mentioned how often he'd been screamed at for doing so. Madeline knew Elizabeth wouldn't like that, so she asked him to write his name in her notebook that had her name on the front, so she could tell her mom. But as he saw her name, he realized that she was the TV host's daughter.

Now inside, Harriet and Madeline were sitting in the front row. Madeline was beaming with pride and joy at seeing her mother in this way but also jealous of sharing her with the eager and intently listening audience.

During a commercial break, Harriet and Madeline were pulled to Walter's office, where he explained that they shouldn't be there because Elizabeth wanted to protect

Madeline from the public eye, given how famous the show and Elizabeth now were.

He also thought to himself how he considered Elizabeth his best friend and, being as close as they were, he noticed how depressed she was despite the success of the show.

Madeline asked why her mother was so famous, and Walter replied that it was because she was so honest and blunt, which was rare to see. At the same time, Elizabeth had taken a question from the audience about what prayer she said before dinner, and to stay true to Walter's words, she answered by saying she's an atheist.

Chapter 33: Faith

Walter received calls of outrage at what Elizabeth said, threatening violence and losing sponsors. Elizabeth couldn't understand the illogicality of this behavior. In her mind, if she respected their belief in God, could they not respect her nonbelief? But the reality was people were irrational and contradictory, seen in matters relating not only to religion but also to sexism and homophobia, things weren't so straightforward.

When the next episode aired, Miss Frask was watching while working. She'd been employed as a typist at Reverend Wakely's office. Elizabeth explained how each person was nearly exactly identical in terms of DNA make-up and therefore found discrimination preposterous, and shared her support for Rosa Parks and the civil rights movement.

She took a question from a woman in the audience who asked what she could eat to lose weight even though she was already taking diet pills. Elizabeth advised against taking the pills and suggested exercising, like rowing, which brought back memories of Calvin.

On a different day, Madeline met Wakely at the park, who was surprised to see her mother on television. He informed her that he eventually got a hold of All Saints, but they had no documents on Calvin Evans. He deduced that it wasn't the correct home, but Madeline was sure it was and that they'd lied.

Chapter 34: All Saints

New and revised characters

- Wilson: the rich man and part of the Parker Foundation that funded the orphanage

- Avery Parker: head of the Parker Foundation

The chapter starts in 1933 with a bishop being assigned to a boys' home as punishment for insulting the archbishop, with the promise that if he secured continuous financial backing, he'd be given a better opportunity. However, four years later, he'd made no progress on their finances despite his efforts of trying to find an endowment—a gift of funding to support the home.

In the present day, the bishop instructed his secretary to lie to the caller that wanted to know about Calvin Evans—Wakely—and say that he'd never lived there. He told the secretary that if the caller persisted, to say that Calvin Evans had been at a different home that burned down.

He remembered how years ago, Calvin regularly got into trouble and how no one was interested in him until a man named Wilson from a wealthy Catholic foundation appeared. Wilson wanted to take Calvin away with him to a few still-living relatives, but the bishop lied, saying Calvin was dead. The bishop knew that the school would receive a donation in memory of Calvin, so he lied to get the money. Wilson seemed shocked and sorrowful at the news and handed over a check for Calvin's "memorial fund" (Garmus, 2022, p. 302).

Years later, when Calvin had grown up and become famous, the head of the foundation, Avery Parker, found out that he was alive and threatened legal action against the home.

Wakely called the orphanage again but pretended to be a potential British sponsor interested in Calvin Evan's childhood orphanage. Ironically, he was lying to find out the truth. The bishop and Wakely talked about the fake donation, but the bishop insisted that Calvin Evans was never at All Saints until Wakely mentioned donating a large amount of money. Hilariously, the bishop's favorite program, *Supper at Six*, was about to start, so he rushed to tell the truth that Calvin had grown up there and that they had a memorial fund for him.

Wakely caught Madeline up to speed when they next met, but she was sharp and questioned why a memorial fund was being funded nine years *before* her dad's death. Wakely had just thought it was a fund to honor Calvin before he died, but despite shrugging off her observation, he gave her the Parker Foundation's post office box address.

Chapter 35: The Smell of Failure

As Elizabeth was on her way to row, she saw many women gathering at the boathouse. Women all over the country were inspired to learn to row after Elizabeth suggested rowing as an exercise on the show

Dr. Mason was irritated that after years of trying to convince his wife to row, Elizabeth had done it in one sentence. He'd been calling Elizabeth for days to discuss how his patients in labor were too enraptured with her show to push.

In the KCTV parking lot, there were hateful protesters angry at Elizabeth's atheism. She'd also received death threats, but Walter didn't inform her, as he knew she'd want to handle it herself.

At home, Six-thirty noticed an unhappy audience member who didn't clap during the show. He hitchhiked on a truck to get to KCTV studios and played dead in front of the security, Seymour, to get inside. Seymour thought Six-thirty came with Harriet and Madeline and accidentally revealed to Elizabeth that the two had come to secretly watch the show live months before.

When she confronted Walter about this, he lied and said it was a school project where Madeline had to see her mom working. While Walter's mind was elsewhere, he unknowingly agreed to let Six-thirty on the show.

Six-thirty quickly became a fan favorite to everyone but Walter. Many episodes later, Six-thirty was surveying the crowd for the one unsmiling audience member he'd seen before. He spotted her and went into the crowd, suddenly smelling nitroglycerin, the smell of the bombs he was forced to find years ago. Despite his trauma, he was able to retrieve the homemade bomb from the woman's bag and put it on Seymour's desk.

Seymour was hailed as a hero for saving the studio. The same reporter from Calvin's funeral wrote a story about it and was surprised to hear that a cooking show was receiving death and bomb threats.

Chapter 36: *Life* and Death

New characters

- Franklin Roth: a reporter at Life magazine

One of the many times Walter and his daughter were dining at the Zott residence, he revealed that *Life* magazine wanted a front cover story on Elizabeth. Elizabeth declined until Walter mentioned he'd also called *Chemistry Today*; the magazine Calvin had appeared in.

He said they weren't interested in a TV show cook, which upset Elizabeth. Walter confided in Harriet about hurting Elizabeth, and the two shared a heartfelt moment when he said Amanda adored her.

Behind the scenes, Harriet managed to convince Elizabeth to do the interview. The magazine reporter, Franklin Roth, was instructed to not bring up Calvin Evans and only focus on Elizabeth's accomplishments. He sat in the live audience and interviewed some of the mostly female viewers. One said the show made her feel like she was "being taken seriously" (Garmus, 2022, p. 323) and commented on how men wouldn't last one day being a woman.

In the interview, Elizabeth didn't respond kindly to Roth's questions about her pants or hairdo. He asked about the pencil in her hair, and she replied coldly. He was about to leave, but Elizabeth decided to take him and the photographer to her house to be more in her element.

They were shown the erg, and she demonstrated how Six-thirty helped her in the home lab. She explained her work in abiogenesis, and even the non-scientific Roth was interested, but she revealed she no longer pursued it. To press further, he asked about Calvin.

She thought he was more interested in Calvin's work than hers and was thoroughly disappointed. Roth regretted asking and wanted to apologize but didn't. She suddenly did the unexpected and told him the entire truth of everything—her parents and brother, Dr. Meyers's assault, Donatti's plagiarism, and Calvin's death.

Chapter 37: Sold Out

Roth started his article by calling Elizabeth "the most influential, intelligent person on television" (Garmus, 2022, p. 329).

In the interview, Elizabeth reminisced how she and Calvin were made for each other and how he thought of her work as just as important as his own, adding that Donatti fully plagiarized her work in his latest paper.

She explained that teaching women chemistry helped them understand the basics of matter—atoms—so that they could identify the foundation of the restrictions placed on them by society. She suggested that religion allowed people to be ignorant and not be held accountable for the problems they'd caused because they could just pray for improvement instead of proactively doing it themselves.

The rest of her life was unraveled: being assaulted at university, her parents' cons, and her brother's suicide.

Calvin's childhood and his misfortunes were also mentioned: his parents and aunt dying and being abused at the boys' home. What she didn't say is that she knew from Calvin's childhood diary that his lifelong grudge was against his father.

Elizabeth told Roth that she blamed herself entirely for Calvin's death. She hated that she'd given up her research because of Donatti, put Madeline in a school she felt excluded in, and become a "performer" like her fraud of a father dreamed of being (Garmus, 2022, p. 334).

After everything, Roth decided to not repeat anything she said and instead wrote about abiogenesis. His editor replaced "intelligent" in his opening sentence with "attractive" (Garmus, 2022, p. 335).

He'd gathered quotes from her father, Dr. Meyers, Donatti, and Mrs. Mudford, who all discredited and insulted her. She'd been called the "devil's spawn" by her father, said to be "more interested in men than molecules" by Meyers, and labeled "disruptive" of her daughter's welfare because she wasn't fulfilling the conservative role of a woman according to Mudford (Garmus, 2022, p. 335).

Roth also included Madeline's family tree in the article, courtesy of Mudford. Madeline had added Walter to the tree—sparking a scandal between Elizabeth and him—and a drawing of Harriet trying to kill her husband with poison, her father's gravestone, and false relations between her and historical figures.

Chapter 38: Brownies

In July 1961, after the degrading magazine was published, Walter was trying to cheer Elizabeth up with marketing offers, like a chemistry toy for girls. She was interested until he mentioned it was stereotypically pink and for making perfume.

Weeks later on the show, Elizabeth was about to explain eggplant facts for that night's dinner but chose to spontaneously bake brownies instead. She'd made brownies five times in a row for supper for her and Madeline because it made her feel better on her awful days—which she was having a lot of.

At home, Harriet abruptly left Madeline alone to watch her mom on TV until Wakely rang the doorbell. He was concerned about Madeline after the magazine was published and wanted to check on her.

Elizabeth came home early and found them talking. Her show was playing on the questions segment. Before she could turn it off, a lady asked if it was true that her daughter was illegitimate—meaning born out of wedlock.

Wakely turned to leave but was stopped by Elizabeth. He apologized for not introducing himself at the funeral and explained he didn't ever meet Calvin but admired him all the same. To Madeline, he stated that illegitimacy was only important to stupid people.

He mentioned how he agreed with Elizabeth that "society" was "based on myth" (p. 343) but she said that wasn't published in the magazine.

This made him realize the reason for his visit—Roth had left a letter for Elizabeth, Madeline had read it, taken it to Wakely, and he was there to deliver it. Madeline cried as she'd read the horrible article and felt responsible because of her family tree.

The letter had a note saying Roth had resigned and was trying to get a truthful article about her published. That new article was in the letter and talked honorably of her achievements and other female scientists.

Despite the flattering article, Madeline was upset because she felt it was her fault that Elizabeth had to be a TV cook and not a chemist; Miss Frask had told her that she was to blame. Elizabeth insisted she was still a chemist, and Madeline asserted that she wasn't.

Chapter 39: Dear Sirs

Two days prior, Madeline met Miss Frask at Wakely's office. Madeline asked about her mom and dad, and Frask said they were in love. It was the first time her words weren't tainted by envy.

Frask thought back to her jealous gossip that resulted in Elizabeth's termination. It led to Elizabeth coming back, her and Frask admitting their assaults and unfinished educations to each other, which resulted in their unfulfilling Hastings jobs.

She tried to soften the truth of what happened, which Madeline hated, so Frask told her that Elizabeth was fired because she was pregnant with Madeline. Madeline was devastated by this, thinking she was to blame for her mother losing her job as a scientist. Madeline gave Frask Roth's letter to Wakely, but Frask ended up reading it.

After reading about Elizabeth's accomplishments in the letter, Frask wrote to *Life* magazine's editors, laying out the truth of Donatti's plagiarism and lies and Elizabeth's mistreatment at Hastings.

Frask's letter was published alongside many other women's supportive letters in the next issue, but Elizabeth didn't care. She was depressed and struggling to continue on. She was used to just carrying on through all her life's tragedies, but she didn't know if she could this time. The magazine had permanently hurt and demotivated her. She shockingly told Harriet that no one was interested in "women in science" (Garmus, 2022, p. 350).

Elizabeth went to work, and it's apparent that this is where Chapter 1 took place.

Harriet blamed herself for Elizabeth's depression because she'd convinced her to do the interview, but as she thought about what Elizabeth said—that no one was interested in scientific women—she had an idea.

Chapter 40: Normal

Elizabeth confessed to Wakely that death often occupied her thoughts and that she thought it was abnormal. He said he was the same and that there may be no such thing as normal. Despite him being a preacher, he implied he didn't believe everything in the Bible.

Elizabeth admitted she'd read the letters between him and Calvin and that Calvin chose to work in Commons because Wakely praised the weather. Wakely felt responsible because he had influenced Calvin's decisions that led to his death. The themes of guilt and responsibility are ever present in the survivors of Calvin's death.

He remembered when Madeline and he shared secrets at the end of Chapter 28. She'd whispered that Six-thirty knew nearly a thousand words, which he didn't believe, and he told her that he didn't believe in God.

Elizabeth told Wakely that her brother had saved her when she leaped into a quarry when she was very young. She felt guilty that she couldn't save him like he'd saved her before he died. Wakely said that suicide wasn't comparable to what he did, but she revealed that he couldn't swim either when he saved her.

Wakely explained that things happen out of one's control, and all one can do is accept them. He told her that being a chemist meant implementing change and praised how she challenged the norm and didn't accept the "unacceptable" (Garmus, 2022, p. 356)—being Calvin and her brother's death—but the reality was permanent things had to be accepted eventually.

She expressed her will to escape and go "out" like her brother, but Wakely speculated that what she actually wanted was to get back "in" (Garmus, 2022, p. 356).

This may mean that her feelings of despair weren't necessarily because she wanted to die but rather because she couldn't see a way out of her depression. She wanted to "get back in" and feel the vigor for life and science she had before Calvin died. She had so much more to do—*to prove*—but she felt lost in how to go about it. It appears that Wakely's words got through to Elizabeth, shown by her actions in the next chapter.

Chapter 41: Recommit

Elizabeth went to Walter's house one night and was shocked to see Harriet with him. He explained that they'd been seeing each other, and Elizabeth hadn't noticed. Elizabeth told them that she was resigning from the show. Harriet and Walter cried but were supportive and hugged her.

The next day, Elizabeth informed everyone watching *Supper at Six* that it would be her last episode. Everyone was in disbelief.

Elizabeth explained she was returning to pursuing chemistry and that she was proud that over the last two years, she and her viewers had created history. She read out a letter from the woman from Chapter 29 who wanted to be an open heart surgeon and stated she'd completed her studies and was well on her way to success. For probably the first time ever on the show, Elizabeth smiled.

Elizabeth wrote "CHEMISTRY IS CHANGE" (Garmus, 2022, p. 360) on her easel, prompted by what Wakely said in the previous chapter. She encouraged women across the country to never allow themselves to be defined by their race, gender, religion, or social class and to forever remember that bravery was the foundation of change.

She thanked Harriet for the advice that she'd given her when they first met, which inspired her ending tagline, and for helping Elizabeth reconsider her own wants and needs that led to her decision to leave the show. Elizabeth had rekindled her spirit and purpose.

She ended the show with a line Walter quickly made up on the spot, acknowledging the cooking show for what it really was at its core: an introductory class to chemistry.

Walter being the one that came up with her last line on the show, reveals his immense character growth. He went from desperately trying to convince Elizabeth to adhere to Phil's superficial vision to now fully leaning into the educational aspect of the show.

Chapter 42: Personnel

Many people, including Elizabeth, expected her to have countless job offers once the show ended. However, Donatti and Meyers's words had left an indelible mark on Elizabeth's scientific reputation. She was only wanted by the public as the host of *Supper at Six*.

Harriet suggested that Elizabeth could go back to the show, but Elizabeth refused. Harriet said that she was on her way to her attorney, presumably to finalize her divorce from Mr. Sloane, but before she left, she mentioned that the director of Personnel at Hastings—Miss Frask—had called for Elizabeth. Elizabeth assumed Frask had been kidding Harriet, as Frask was dismissed years ago.

Elizabeth called back and was surprised to find that it was all true. Frask was now the head of the department she'd been fired from and was asking Elizabeth to come in because the rich sponsor had resurfaced after he'd seen Frask's letter to *Life* magazine.

Harriet thought back to all the times she confessed her husband's abuse to the priest, and the priest told *her* to change for him so he'd stop hurting her. She'd tried to heed his advice using magazines, but after she met Elizabeth, she realized that she didn't need to change anything about herself. She decided to pursue a career in magazines, starting with Roth's unused article. This was the idea she had at the end of Chapter 39.

At Hastings, Elizabeth met the secretary and was asked to sign her newest magazine. Confused, Elizabeth examined the magazine that had recently published Roth's article—thanks to Harriet.

Elizabeth met the sponsor—Avery Parker and Wilson—in Calvin's lab at their insistence. They asked her to continue her research at Hastings, but Elizabeth immediately declined.

Suddenly, Donatti barged into the lab, acknowledging only Wilson and sneering at Avery, Frask, and Elizabeth. Wilson explained they knew of his deceit and swindling of their money. Donatti tried to blame Frask's letter and threatened to sue, but Wilson revealed he was her lawyer. Avery candidly handed Donatti a notice of termination, giving him the same dismissive tone he'd given Elizabeth all those years ago.

He was astonished, and more so at the news that Elizabeth was to take over his job as the new head of Chemistry. She was given the power to let him stay or go, and as satisfying payback, she told him that he simply wasn't smart enough.

Chapter 43: Stillborn

As Donatti was ushered out, Avery explained that she wasn't married, like Elizabeth.

Elizabeth said that she knew their foundation was interested in funding religious institutions like orphanages. Wilson responded that while their founders had been interested in religion, they'd also turned their attention to science, especially because of her and Calvin.

Elizabeth remembered the description of the rich man in Calvin's diary—identical to Wilson. She asked if they'd ever supplied educational materials to a boys' home in Iowa.

At this mention, Avery asked Wilson to leave so she could speak with Elizabeth alone, but Elizabeth wanted to ask Wilson questions.

Elizabeth thought that they had feigned the job offer to get to Calvin's belongings and that Wilson was Calvin's hated biological father. Avery said Wilson had no children and was just her lawyer and the "face" of the foundation (Garmus, 2022, p. 374).

Avery wasn't afforded the right to inherit her foundation since she was a woman and had to have her nonexistent husband's approval, so she'd signed on Wilson as a trustee to help her act as the head.

Elizabeth accused them of only being after Calvin's items, and Avery felt regretful as the misunderstanding furthered.

Avery told the tale of a seventeen-year-old girl who became pregnant after falling in love. Her religious parents sent her off to a jail-like home for pregnant and unmarried women. She was told she had to sign to give her baby away, but she refused and was forced to go through labor alone. A doctor tired of the noise and went to anesthetize her, and she woke up to the news that her baby was stillborn. Ten years later, a nurse from the home was bribed by the woman and told her that her baby was alive, and she started looking for him.

Avery was Calvin's biological mother.

Chapter 44: The Acorn

After the shocking revelation, Elizabeth remembered the letters from the one relentless 'mother' who continuously wrote to Calvin. Avery told Elizabeth that she'd sent Wilson to the home because she was just as wary of scams as her son. Wilson was informed of Calvin's apparent death, and Elizabeth pieced together that it was done for money.

Avery asked her if she'd ever lost someone, and Elizabeth replied that she'd lost her brother to suicide. To this, Avery woefully commented on how they both knew what it was like to be responsible for a loved one's death.

Avery felt as if she'd buried Calvin twice: once by financing his fake memorial and again when he died. She was an atheist, like Elizabeth, but not because of science but because the church had ripped her son away from her and told her that he was dead.

She gave the home educational materials and rowing lessons to honor him because his biological father was a rower. This was how Calvin learned to row and was able to attend Cambridge University.

The truth was revealed to her when Calvin appeared on a magazine cover, but Avery decided to let him find out the truth in his own time by writing him letters. She realized now that she shouldn't have been so patient.

Avery gathered that Calvin and Elizabeth were together from the rumors at Hastings, which was why Wilson strictly funded abiogenesis—and also because Avery enjoyed the precarious position it placed Donatti in.

Wilson knew Elizabeth was a woman and had planned to meet her in person, but then Calvin suddenly died. Avery thought that Elizabeth wasn't close to Calvin from the misconstruing articles surrounding his death and their relationship.

Avery was at the funeral but was unable to meet Elizabeth because Elizabeth had left so quickly. She assumed Elizabeth didn't love him, but she cried out that she did entirely and never stopped loving him. They sobbed in grief and hugged each other.

Chapter 45: Supper at Six

Six-thirty noticed the deep connection the two women had as they hugged. Avery admitted to Elizabeth that she knew very little of Calvin's life until she'd received a letter in her post office box from Madeline. Thanks to Madeline's information, Avery was able to ascertain the truth—her death had been faked because of her defiance in the womens' home, and the bishop had shown Calvin her "death certificate."

Avery showed Elizabeth a picture of Calvin's biological father, who looked nearly identical to him. He'd died of tuberculosis before Calvin was born. He met Avery by accident when he rode over her with his bike, and she always wore a brooch he'd gifted her.

Elizabeth explained that her and Calvin's meeting wasn't love at first sight but promised she'd tell Avery more about him in the future. Elizabeth welcomed her as part of the family and remarked that the acorn on Madeline's family tree was actually *her* and not Wilson.

Wilson interrupted as he and Avery had to leave soon to deal with more business before their departure the next day.

Wanting Avery to stay for a bit longer, Elizabeth invited her and Wilson to "supper at six" (Garmus, 2022, p. 386) at her home to meet the family—Walter, Harriet, her, and Madeline, and eventually Wakely and Dr. Mason too. Avery sincerely accepted before she left.

The novel ends with Six-thirty informing the readers that he knew Avery was Calvin's mother at 2:42 p.m.—which is what he'll call her—and picking up an untouched notebook so that Elizabeth could resume her abiogenesis research.

Dear Reader

I want to personally thank you for choosing this book from among dozens out there, for acquiring an authorized copy of it and supporting my work, and for making it all the way to the end.

If you liked the content, please consider posting a review or rating on Amazon, it would mean a lot to me and it would help others benefit from my work. It is also the best way to support independent writers like myself.

Thank you,

Alice & Liam

References

Garmus, B. (2022). *Lessons in Chemistry*. Doubleday.

Made in United States
Orlando, FL
29 November 2023

39786729R00064